Raintree is an imprint of Capstone Global Library Limited, a
company incorporated in England and Wales having its registered
office at 7 Pilgrim Street, London, EC4V 6LB – Registered
company number: 6695582

"Raintree" is a registered trademark of Pearson Education
Limited, under licence to Capstone Global Library Limited

Art Director: Heather Kinseth
Cover Graphic Designer: Brann Garvey
Interior Graphic Designer: Kay Fraser, Brann Garvey
Edited in the UK by Laura Knowles
Printed and bound in China by Leo Paper Products Ltd

ISBN 978-1406212679 (hardback)
13 12 11 10 09
10 9 8 7 6 5 4 3 2 1

ISBN 978-1406212815 (paperback)
14 13 12 11 10
10 9 8 7 6 5 4 3 2 1

British Library Cataloguing in Publication Data
Dahl, Michael.
The beast beneath the stairs. -- (Library of doom)
813.5'4-dc22
A full catalogue record for this book is available
from the British Library.

TABLE OF CONTENTS

 he Library of Doom is the world's largest collection of strange and dangerous books. The Librarian's duty is to keep the books from falling into the hands of those who would use them for evil purposes.

4

CHAPTER 1

THE DARK LIBRARY

The **Library of Doom** is dark.

The stairways are silent.

Cobwebs hang across the doors.

The Library's gardens are filled with weeds and **creeping** vines.

Floors are covered with broken glass.

Somewhere, boots **crunch** on the broken glass.

A shadow walks through the hallways.

It is the **Librarian**.

CHAPTER 2

THE
LIBRARIAN

He is cold and tired, but he is glad to be home.

The Librarian looks down at his hands.

The Librarian has come back
with a handful of new books.

The Librarian has been gone for
a long time.

He has travelled over mountains and crossed deserts of ice.

He has fought many battles with strange creatures.

He has discovered books that no one else has seen for hundreds of years.

The books are filled with terrible powers.

Now, the Librarian is home.

The Librarian smiles. He is looking forward to being in his own place.

He is looking forward to having a long rest.

He passes through a **huge** door and walks up the stairs towards his room.

The moonlight makes strange shadows on the stairs.

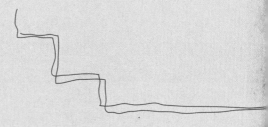

When he reaches the top step, the
Librarian frowns. He makes a fist.

The door to his room
has been ripped away.

CHAPTER 3

THE MISSING BOOKS

The Librarian runs through the hole in the door.

He enters his room.

A wind blows
across the pages of
his books and papers.
The window has been
smashed.

A  has
been here.

The Librarian runs
to a special shelf where
he keeps his most
dangerous books.

The lock is smashed.
The books are missing.

The Librarian knows that one of his **powerful enemies** has taken the books.

Scattered pages lead up a stairway. They are pages from the missing books.

"I must find the books," the Librarian tells himself, "or the world is in `terrible danger`."

The pages pass out of a window and curve down into the **deep darkness**.

(CHAPTER 4)

BENEATH THE STAIRS

The Librarian stands on the sill of his window.

He puts his hands at his side, takes a deep breath, and jumps.

He falls through the air like a
heavy book.

The Librarian falls through rooms
that he has forgotten.

Staircases and balconies flash
past him. Statues stare at him.

After many minutes, the
Librarian lands at the very bottom
of the library.

His boots scrape against old stones.

He follows the trail of pages
through **twisting halls**.

When he turns a corner, the
Librarian sees a great hole in the
wall. The trail of pages disappears
into the hole.

In front of the hole crouches
a beast made of books.

CHAPTER 5

THE BEAST OF BOOKS

The beast is part man and part book and part octopus. The creature made of three parts roars.

Its long tongue rolls out. Its long arms unfold like hundreds of pages.

The Librarian jumps back.

Then the creature shoots out **`jets of ink`**. A cloud of darkness fills the room and blinds the Librarian.

From behind him, long arms grab his waist.

The Librarian is **squeezed** by the creature's powerful arms.

Quickly, the Librarian holds up
his hands.

A **powerful light** flashes
from his fingers. A blast of heat rips
through the `inky cloud`.

The beast crumples into torn
pieces of paper.

The Librarian closes his 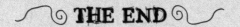.
He takes a deep breath and then
stands up.

He must find the missing books.

He steps into the dark hole.

∿ THE END ∿

A PAGE FROM
THE LIBRARY
OF DOOM

LIBRARIES

The British Library in London contains
more than 150 million items, including
books, maps, newspapers, and drawings.

The world's most overdue library book
was borrowed from a British university in
1668. The book was returned in 1956 but
no fine was charged!

The Library of Alexandria in Egypt
was considered the greatest library of
ancient times. It held more than 700,000
rolls of paper, which is how books were
written then.

In 1731, Benjamin Frankin opened the world's first "members only" library. Thanks to Ben, people still use library cards.

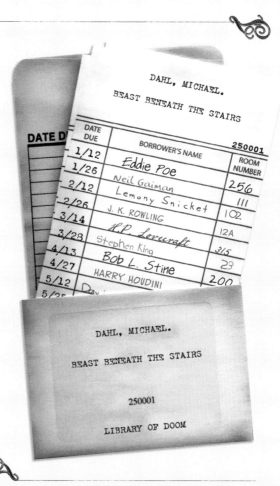

DAHL, MICHAEL.

BEAST BENEATH THE STAIRS

DATE DUE	BORROWER'S NAME	250001
DATE DUE	BORROWER'S NAME	ROOM NUMBER
1/12	Eddie Poe	
1/26	Neil Gaiman	256
2/12	Lemony Snicket	111
2/26	J. K. ROWLING	102
3/14	H.P. Lovecraft	12A
3/28	Stephen King	315
4/13	Bob L. Stine	23
4/27	HARRY HOUDINI	200
5/12	Da...	
5/25		

DAHL, MICHAEL.

BEAST BENEATH THE STAIRS

250001

LIBRARY OF DOOM

ABOUT THE AUTHOR

Michael Dahl is the author of more than
100 books for children and young adults.
He has twice won the AEP Distinguished
Achievement Award for his non-fiction. His
Finnegan Zwake mystery series was chosen
by the Agatha Awards to be among the
five best mystery books for children in 2002
and 2003. He collects books on poison and
graveyards, and lives in a haunted house in
Minneapolis, USA.

ABOUT THE ILLUSTRATOR

Patricia Moffett loves fantasy and horror. In
fact, the building where she works in London
was built by the man who designed the scary
house in the classic 1963 ghost film, *The
Haunting*. Moffett used the building as the
inspiration for her illustrations of the Library
of Doom. She enjoys designing book covers
and reading mythology and science fiction.

GLOSSARY

balconies (BAL-kuh-neez) – platforms on the outside of a building. Balconies are usually high above the ground and have railings.

clinging (KLING-ing) – holding on tightly

creeping (KREEP-ing) – growing and spreading over a surface, like a vine

crumple (KRUM-pul) – to shrink and break down, like an empty balloon

twisted (TWIS-tid) – curved and turning, bent out of shape

DISCUSSION QUESTIONS

1. The Librarian keeps the most dangerous books in the world locked up in his library. What do you think makes these books so dangerous? Can a book really be dangerous? Explain.

2. The Library of Doom is the largest library in the world. It is also the strangest. Would you want to visit it? Why or why not? Would you go alone, or would you want someone to go with you?

3. At the end of the story, the Librarian steps through the hole in the wall. Where is he going? What do you think happens next?

WRITING PROMPTS

1. The Librarian has returned to the Library of Doom after many adventures and battles. The author gives a few clues about what might have happened during those travels. Write your own story describing one of the Librarian's unknown adventures.

2. The beast beneath the stairs is made of books. Draw a picture of a creature made from objects you might find in a classroom. Then write a description of the creature. What does it eat? How does it sleep? Is it dangerous or tame? Does it make noises? How does it smell?

MORE BOOKS TO READ

This story may be over, but there are many
more dangerous adventures in store for the
Librarian. Will the Librarian be able to escape
the cave of the deadly giant bookworms? Will
he defeat the rampaging Word Eater in time
to save the world? You can only find out by
reading the other books from the Library of
Doom...